HOPSCOTCH
TWISTY TALES

Snow White
Sees the Light

by Karen Wallace and Andy Rowland

W
FRANKLIN WATTS
LONDON•SYDNEY

This story is based on the traditional fairy tale,
Snow White and the Seven Dwarfs,
but with a new twist. You can read the original
story in Hopscotch Fairy Tales. Can you make
up your own twist for the story?

First published in 2012 by
Franklin Watts
338 Euston Road
London
NW1 3BH

Franklin Watts Australia
Level 17/207 Kent Street
Sydney
NSW 2000

Text © Karen Wallace 2012
Illustrations © Andy Rowland 2012

The rights of Karen Wallace to be identified as the author
and Andy Rowland as the illustrator of this Work have been asserted
in accordance with the Copyright, Designs and Patents Act, 1988.

A CIP catalogue record for this book is available
from the British Library.
ISBN 978 1 4451 0670 0 (hbk)
ISBN 978 1 4451 0676 2 (pbk)

Series Editor: Melanie Palmer
Series Advisor: Catherine Glavina
Series Designer: Peter Scoulding

Printed in China

Franklin Watts is a division of
Hachette Children's Books,
an Hachette UK company
www.hachette.co.uk

Snow White put down
her broom and sighed.

Every day the seven dwarfs left muddy boots in the kitchen and dropped their jackets on the floor.

5

They never took off their hats.

They only wanted to be fed.

"What's cooking?"

"I'm starving!"

"Hurry up!"

When they sat at the table, the
dwarfs had terrible manners.

And they never ever cleaned
the table or helped with
the washing up.

9

One day, Snow White lost her temper. "All you want is a housekeeper," she cried. "You don't care about me!"

The dwarfs stared at her
in amazement.

11

"But we adore you," said one.

"You are the loveliest in the land," cried another.

"We'd be lost without you!" said a third.

"Huh," muttered Snow White,
but she went to put a pie in
the oven anyway.

Far away, a wise Queen lived
in a castle. She believed that
everyone in her kingdom should
share the cooking and cleaning.

That way everyone would
be happy.

One day, the Queen picked up
her magic mirror.
"Mirror, mirror in my hand, does
someone need me in my land?"

"Snow White needs you," replied the mirror straight away. "The seven dwarfs are treating her like a slave."

The Queen visited Snow White.
"Why do you let the dwarfs
get away with it?" she asked.

"They say they'd be lost without me," replied Snow White.

"We'll see about that." said the Queen. She cut out a piece from a magic apple.

"Pretend you've been poisoned
and see what the dwarfs say when
they find you."

That evening, the seven dwarfs marched in the door, threw off their boots and shouted for their supper.

Then they saw Snow White
lying on the floor with the
apple beside her.

"Oh, no!" cried the dwarfs. "That apple is poisoned! Snow White is dead!" They all burst into tears.

"Who's going to cook our food?"

"Who's going to clean our house?"

"Who's going to wash our clothes?"

Snow White got up from the floor
and gave the seven dwarfs
a long, hard stare.

"Wash your own dishes!" she said.
"I'm leaving!"

And guess what? Snow White found a nice prince and lived very happily ever after.

Puzzle 1

Put these pictures in the correct order.
Which event do you think is most important?
Now try writing the story in your own words!

Puzzle 2

Choose the correct speech bubbles for each
character. Can you think of any others?
Turn over to find the answers.

Answers

Puzzle 1

The correct order is: 1f, 2d, 3e, 4a, 5c, 6b

Puzzle 2

Snow White: 2, 3

The seven dwarfs: 5, 6

The Queen: 1, 4

*hardback

For more Hopscotch books go to:
www.franklinwatts.co.uk